PURIM PLAY

by Roni Schotter Illustrated by Marylin Hafner

Cast

Frannie . . . . as Queen Esther

Ezra . . . . as Mordechai, Esther's Older Cousin

David. . . . . as King Ahasueras

The part of the evil Haman will be played by a mystery guest.

Special Effects. . . . . Rachel and Daniel, Noisemakers

WELCOME TO ALL

REFRESHMENTS WILL BE SERVED.

Amazon Children's Publishing

Also by Roni Schotter and Marylin Hafner:

Hanukkah!
Passover Magic

For the Ripps/Kogen Family—Linda Ripps, Rabbi Avram Kogen, Navah, and Seffi—with appreciation
—R.S.

For Katherine and Irving
—M.H.

JEWISH BEDTIME STORIES and SONGS
www.pjlibrary.org

PJ Library is an international, award-winning program created by the Harold Grinspoon Foundation to support families on their Jewish journeys. To learn more about PJ Library, visit www.pjlibrary.org.

Amazon Publishing
Attn: Amazon Children's Publishing
P.O.Box 400818
Las Vegas, NV 89149
www.amazon.com/amazonchildrenspublishing

The illustrations are rendered in ink and watercolor.

Printed in China (R)
3 5 6 4

Library of Congress Cataloging-in-Publication Data

Schotter, Roni.
Purim play / Roni Schotter ; [illustrated by] Marylin Hafner.
p. cm.
Summary: Frannie is upset because an elderly neighbor is going to play the part of Haman in this year's Purim play, but Mrs. Teplitzky surprises everyone with her acting ability. Includes facts about Purim and a recipe for hamantaschen, a traditional Purim pastry.
ISBN 978-0-7614-5800-5
[1. Purim--Fiction. 2. Theater—Fiction. 3. Fasts and feasts—Judaism—Fiction.] I. Hafner, Marylin, ill. II. Title.
PZ7.S3765Pu 2010
[E]—dc22
2010001538

Every year when we are winter weary and longing for spring, Purim comes! Outside, the March wind huffs and puffs and blows itself out while, inside, *we* huff and puff, out of breath from practicing for our Purim play.

Last night we wore our costumes to synagogue to hear the story of Purim read. Today we add last-minute decorations. I sit on the floor between my big brother, Ezra, and my baby sister, Rachel, a Purim noisemaker who loves to giggle and scream.

I paint circles of color on one of my mother's old robes, then paste down beads that sparkle like stars. Ezra snips a crown from silver foil. In our play, he likes to play the king with the name that sounds like a sneeze: Ahasueras! That way he gets to order everyone around. I don't mind, because *I* play Queen Esther. She's the brave and clever one, and *she* saves the Jewish people.

Megan's Books Boston

But *this* year, there may not be a play. Our cousins who always act out the other two characters in the Purim story have the flu! Ezra has a friend named David who says he will come and act in our play, but only if Ezra lets *him* be the king. So, this Purim, Ezra will play Esther's cousin Mordechai instead. But who will play the villain Haman, the wicked man who tried to murder all the Jews? We need one more person. Without a Haman, there's no story.

"Maybe Papa will do it," I say, sniffing a trail to the kitchen, warm and sweet with baking smells.

"Do what, Frannie?" my father asks, his nose dusted with flour. He and my mother are preparing our Purim party, carrying long trays of glasses and laying out freshly baked hamantaschen, special Purim pastries: prune, poppy seed, and Mama's famous "bet-you-can't-eat-just-one" apricot-orange.

"Play Haman," I say. "We need one more person."

"We have a Haman," my mother announces, and before I can ask her what she means, she pops a gluey, delicious hamantasch into my mouth. "I invited Mrs. Teplitzky from up the street to our party," she explains. "She's a widow now and has no one of her own."

Mrs. Teplitzky? I swallow my hamantasch whole. "*She's* going to play Haman? But how can she? She's a grown-up and a woman and —"

"And she's old and she talks funny," Ezra says.

Our father laughs. So does Baby Rachel, even though she doesn't get the joke.

"You're all acting Haman-ish," my mother says, frowning. "Hateful, mean, and nasty. Why can't a woman play a man's part?"

Ezra just sighs while Papa and I feel ashamed. Mama's right, I think. We *are* acting like Haman. But even so, I think, Mrs. *Teplitzky?*

The doorbell rings and David arrives, dressed as the king. He carries his brother Daniel, a baby noisemaker like Rachel. Right away, Daniel and Rachel scream and start tumbling together, like two crazy kittens. Erza hands David the crown he's made, and David helps Ezra put on his Mordechai costume.

And I? I stand by myself in the hallway, suddenly lonely. Ezra has David for a friend, and Rachel has Daniel. But there's no one for me.

Papa sees me sad. "Who can tell?" he whispers. "Crazy and wonderful things happen, especially at Purim. Maybe you and Mrs. Teplitzky can be friends."

Impossible, I think, but I don't say the word out loud.

Instead, I reach for Esther's robe and slip it on. Now I feel better! Stronger. More like a queen.

The bell rings again. Ezra, David, and I know who it is, and not one of us wants to open the door. When finally we do, a bearded Mrs. Teplitzky stands before us. At least we *think* it's Mrs. Teplitzky. We can't be sure because *she* looks so much like a *he!*

"So, I can come in, or not?" she asks in her singsong way, and then we know for sure it's her.

"Of course," I say. "You look . . ." I don't know how to finish.

"Wicked! You can say it. Today I am a wicked, wicked man. So? We should rehearse. But first . . ." She pulls a small zippered bag from somewhere under her robe and leads me into the bathroom. "Esther was not only brave," she says, "she was beauty-full. You could use a little color."

Quicker than you can say "hamantaschen," she colors my lips cherry red, my cheeks strawberry pink, and my eyelids sea green. She puts a long necklace with giant sparkling stones around my neck and slips a matching ring on my finger.

"What do you think, boys?" she asks Ezra and David. "A Purim beauty, no?"

I blush. Ezra and David don't answer. They just roll their eyes.

"So? Time to start the rehearsal." Her voice is suddenly deep and amazingly like a man's. "I am now the evil Haman!" she announces, sounding not a bit like herself. "And so, we begin."

Ezra starts the scene where Mordechai, because he is Jewish, refuses to bow to Haman, the king's evil prime minister. Mrs. Teplitzky stomps around the room, red and furious, shouting angrily in her deep Haman voice. I hate to admit it, but she's a good actor. When she raises her hand high and swears in revenge to murder Mordechai and all the Jews, Rachel and Daniel hide. At last it's my turn.

"Esther," Ezra, as Mordechai, says to me, "you must tell the king about Haman's wicked plan and that you are Jewish. He doesn't know. If you tell him, maybe he'll stop Haman and save our people." Ezra's Mordechai voice is flat, and he speaks slowly, as if he is half asleep.

"More expression!" Mrs. Teplitzky calls out, like a director.

Ezra scowls but tries again. This time, he's better. Now it's up to me.

"But Mordechai," I say, "I'm m-m-much too afraid to tell the king. When he finds out I'm Jewish, he'll kill me." I tremble as I think how frightened the real Esther must have been, how brave she had to be to save the Jewish people.

"Excellent!" Mrs. Teplitzky interrupts.

"Courage," Ezra says, the same way he might say, "Carrots." He's my brother, so I won't tell him, but the truth is, he's a terrible actor.

"Do it the way Frannie does," Mrs. Teplitzky orders. "With feeling."

"How do *you* know so much about acting?" Ezra asks rudely.

But Mrs. Teplitzky is not offended. She takes off her Haman hat, her wig, and beard, and speaks in her regular voice. "Long ago, before any of you were born, I was an actress. I acted here. I acted there. I still have my costumes in an old trunk. This is one of them," she says, pointing proudly to her robe.

"An actress! Could you teach *me* to act?" I ask, and hold my breath.
"Sure. Easy. Already you're a good actress."
"It's true," Ezra says. "Frannie's the actress in *this* family."
"Oh, Ezra," I say, "thank you!"

Out in the hall, there's a commotion. The guests are arriving for our party.
No more time to rehearse. We are all nervous, but our Purim play must go on!

In the living room, we pass out rattles to the baby noisemakers and pots and pans to the grown-ups so that everyone has a grogger — something to bang or shake to make lots of noise whenever they hear Haman-the-horrible's name.

Our play starts off well, and soon we get to the part we haven't rehearsed yet, when Esther cleverly invites King Ahasueras and Haman to a fancy dinner and, with great courage, tells the king that someone is planning to kill her and her people.

"Who is he and where is he that dares this dreadful deed?" David, as Ahasueras, roars in terrible anger. He's pretty good!

"He is," I announce, and then pause and point *very* dramatically, "your prime minister, the terribly wicked . . . *Haman!!!*"

The living room vibrates as everyone boos, hisses, stamps their feet, and shakes their noisemakers at Mrs. Teplitzky. Mrs. Teplitzky, splendidly evil, hisses back. And Rachel and Daniel, the baby noisemakers? They scream, of course. Perfect!

In the exciting finale, Haman is ordered off the stage to be executed and Mordechai is made the new prime minister. I, Queen Esther, have saved the Jewish people!

Daniel and Rachel jump up and down as, to great applause, we actors take our bows. No doubt about it, Mrs. Teplitzky is the best Haman we've ever had!

"Mrs. Teplitzky," I say, suddenly shy. "Tomorrow . . . may I come to your house? . . . Could you show me your costumes?"

"Sure," Mrs. Teplitzky answers. "Together, you and I, we'll act. Okay?"

"Okay!" I shout. My father was right. Mrs. Teplitzky and I are friends! Crazy and wonderful things *do* happen at Purim.

Time for our Purim party, for tea-in-a-glass, and Mama's hamantaschen and more hamantaschen, and still more after that! Our living room bursts with family and friends, old and new. And I? I stand in the center of it, full of happiness, hamantaschen, and the joy of Purim play.

The Story of Purim: The Feast of Lots

Long ago, in the ancient kingdom of Persia, King Ahasueras chose Esther, a young Jewish woman, to be his queen. The king didn't know that Esther was Jewish, and Mordechai, Esther's older cousin and guardian, warned Esther that it was best that she not tell him.

Ahasueras had an evil adviser named Haman, who expected everyone to bow down to him. When Mordechai refused to do so, because his religion forbade him to bow to false idols, Haman became furious. He vowed to kill Mordechai and all the Jews in the kingdom. To choose a date for his terrible crime, Haman cast lots, called *purim* in Hebrew. The lots fell on the thirteenth day of the Hebrew month of Adar.

When Mordechai heard of Haman's evil plan, he told Esther to go before the king, tell him that she was Jewish, and ask him to save her people. But Esther could see the king only if he invited her to do so. To break the law would mean risking her life.

For three days the Jewish people fasted and prayed to give Esther courage. Happily, when brave Esther went to see the king without being invited, he wasn't angry. In fact, he offered to grant her any wish! Esther asked only that the king and Haman attend a special banquet as her guests. The king and Haman came, and Esther promised the king she'd reveal her wish at a *second* banquet on the following night.

At the second banquet, Esther told the king that she was Jewish, that her life and the lives of her people were in danger, and of Haman's wicked plan. Furious, the king ordered Haman hanged on the gallows Haman had built for Mordechai. He gave Mordechai Haman's job. Esther's courage had saved the Jewish people.

Many times, throughout the ages, Jewish people have found themselves in mortal danger simply for practicing their religion. The story of Purim has sustained them — giving them hope that, in the end, just as Esther and Mordechai triumphed over Haman, good can triumph over evil.

How Purim Is Celebrated

Every year, on the thirteenth day of the Hebrew month of Adar, which usually falls in March, Jewish children and adults are encouraged to celebrate the joyous holiday of Purim with noise and merriment. People go to synagogue or a Jewish center to hear the story of Purim read aloud from the Megillah, the Book of Esther, in the Bible. Children dress up in costumes, and everyone uses groggers, or noisemakers, to drown out Haman's name.

At home, people enjoy a festive meal that includes hamantaschen, triangular pastries shaped like Haman's hat or ears. They may decide to put on a Purim play. It is also a custom at Purim to remember others by practicing *mishloah manot,* sending portions of hamantaschen and other sweets to neighbors, friends, or relatives and by performing *tzedakah,* giving gifts of money to anyone in need.

The tradition of a Purim play, or *Purim spiel* in Yiddish, is an old one, dating back to the sixteenth century, when people went from house to house dressed in costumes and performing skits based on the Purim story. Some say the Purim spiel was the beginning of modern Jewish theater. Today, many children enjoy dressing in Purim masquerade costumes and putting on their own Purim plays.

Mama's Famous "Bet-You-Can't-Eat-Just-One" Apricot-Orange Hamantaschen

Make these with adult supervision.

Dough

¼ lb. softened margarine
1 cup sugar
2 eggs
1 teaspoon vanilla
2 cups flour

Filling

apricot preserves
grated orange rind (to taste)

1. Mix dough ingredients in order. Stir in more flour if needed until a ball is formed.
2. Chill the dough in the refrigerator for 2 hours or overnight.
3. On a floured board, roll out the dough to a ¼- to ⅛-inch thickness. Using a round cookie cutter or a glass, cut out circles about 2½ to 3 inches in diameter.
4. Mix the filling ingredients in a small bowl. Put a teaspoon of filling in the center of each circle. Fold the edges of each circle in thirds to form a triangle, and pinch the edges together, leaving a small circle of filling exposed.
5. Bake on a nonstick cookie sheet in a preheated 350-degree oven for 18 minutes or until golden brown. Cool on a wire rack. Makes about 2½ dozen.